Just Stay Put

For my father

Text and illustrations copyright © 1995
by Gary Clement

Groundwood Books/Douglas & McIntyre Ltd.
585 Bloor Street West
Toronto, Ontario M6G 1K5

The publisher gratefully acknowledges the assistance of
the Canada Council, the Ontario Arts Council and the
Ontario Ministry of Culture, Tourism and Recreation.

Canadian Cataloguing in Publication Data

Clement, Gary
Just stay put

ISBN 0-88899-239-4

I. Title.

PS8555.L4J8 1995   jC813'.54   C95-931498-9
PZ7.C54Ju 1995

First published in the United States in 1996
The illustrations are done in pen and ink
and gouache
Design by Michael Solomon
Printed and bound in Hong Kong by
Everbest Printing Co. Ltd.

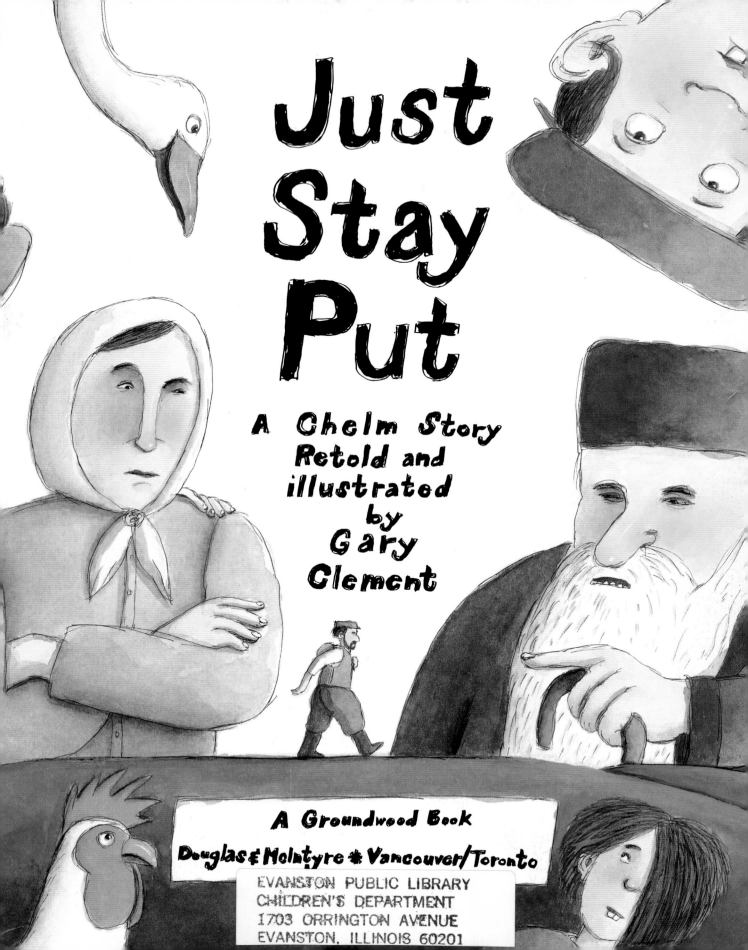

Just
Stay
Put

A Chelm Story
Retold and
illustrated
by
Gary
Clement

A Groundwood Book

Douglas & McIntyre ✱ Vancouver/Toronto

THE little village of Chelm consisted of only a few dozen shaky huts, a main street, an old synagogue, a shabby marketplace. The people of Chelm were like people in villages everywhere. They were hard-working and

honest. They were peasants and peddlers. They were
fishmongers and farmers. They were barbers and
babysitters. They were this and they were that.

They were also extremely silly.

Of course, the good people of Chelm never actually thought of themselves as silly. In fact, they felt they were quite clever—wise, almost. And the villagers believed that their town rabbi was the wisest Chelmite of all, perhaps even the wisest man alive.

So how wise was he? Here's an example.

One day the rabbi was stopped on the main street of Chelm by a group of villagers.

"Rabbi," asked one. "Tell us, which is more important, the sun or the moon?"

"Why, the moon, of course," responded the rabbi immediately. "At night when it's dark out, the moon enables us to see. During the day when it's already light, who needs the sun?"

The rabbi had once again proven to the villagers that a great sage lived within their midst.

Do you want another example of how silly, or clever, the people of Chelm were? Listen.

At one time there lived in Chelm a man named Mendel. He was a good husband and a kind father, but he was also very lazy. All he did all day was dream. He dreamed of being a great genius, capable of solving all the problems of the universe. He dreamed of being able to fly like a bird. But most of all, he dreamed of traveling.

"I've spent my whole life in Chelm," thought Mendel. "I'd like to see a little bit of the world."

Mendel's wife, Malke, was, like Mendel, good and kind. But sometimes she could not help but be angry with Mendel for being such a do-nothing daydreamer.

"Mendel," she would ask, "when will you get a job already?"

"OK, I'll think about it," Mendel would say.

"And when will you be thinking about it?" Malke would ask sharply.

"When I get a job," Mendel would answer calmly.

One day Malke asked Mendel, "Nu, so what are you daydreaming about this day?"

"Traveling," Mendel answered quietly.

"And where exactly will you travel, Mister Big Shot Traveler?" asked Malke mockingly.

"Well, I've always wanted to see Warsaw" replied Mendel.

"And how will you get to Warsaw? Will you fly like a bird?"

"Oh, Malkele, Malkele. If only I could," groaned Mendel.

But the sad fact was that Mendel and Malke were very poor. They barely had enough food to feed their children and the few scraggly geese that they kept in their yard.

"I'm stuck here forever," thought Mendel sadly.

That very night Mendel had a dream. He dreamed he
was in a great town. All around him were magnificent
buildings on streets that stretched as far as the eye could
see. The road teemed with people dressed in the most
fabulous clothes. It was crowded with circus animals and
acrobats, elaborate horseless carriages and vendors sell-
ing everything under the sun.

"Where am I?" asked Mendel dreamily.

"You are in Warsaw, my friend," answered a passerby.

Then Mendel woke up.

"That's it," he decided. "I've got to get to Warsaw, right now, this minute!"

It was still very early in the morning when Mendel quietly got dressed, packed his bag with some bread and an onion, filled his water flask and left his little house.

As the villagers of Chelm rolled this way and that way in their feather beds, Mendel took his first steps along the dusty road to Warsaw.

At first he found the walking pleasant—enjoyable, even. The sun wasn't too hot, the breeze was gentle, and there weren't too many holes in his old boots. But as the day wore on, Mendel wore out. By the time the sun was high in the noon sky, he was ready to stop for some lunch.

He found a shady spot by the side of the road where he sat to eat his modest meal. After eating, he felt an overwhelming urge to nap.

"But if I nap," thought Mendel, "how will I remember which way I was walking when I wake up?" In a flash, he thought of a solution to this tricky problem. He removed

his boots from his feet and placed them near the road, toes pointing to Warsaw.

"This way, even if I forget, my shoes will remember." And with that, Mendel fell into a deep and contented sleep.

As he slept, a poor shepherd passed by with his meager flock. Seeing Mendel's boots, this shepherd said to himself, "I could do with a new pair of boots. Mine are old and full of holes. Maybe I'll switch boots with this sleeping peasant here, and who will be the wiser?"

The sly shepherd picked up Mendel's boots and gave them a thorough inspection.

"These boots have more holes than my own," thought the disappointed shepherd. "Feh! They don't smell too good, either. You can keep your boots, mister!"

So the shepherd dropped Mendel's boots exactly where he'd found them, only now the toes pointed the other way, back to Chelm.

Mendel awoke refreshed and ready to continue his adventurous journey. He eagerly put on his boots without noticing, even for one second, that they had been turned around and that they would take him directly back to Chelm.

As Mendel resumed walking, he noticed that everything he passed looked strangely familiar.

"But how can this be?" he thought. "I've never been on this road before."

Mendel walked on.

As the sun began to set, he approached a small village.

"Can this be Warsaw?" he wondered. "It looks exactly like Chelm from here."

Mendel entered the village. He recognized every building and every person he passed. Not only that, but everyone he passed seemed to recognize him!

"Hello, Reb Mendel," said someone who looked exactly like Pinchas Garfinkel, the butcher.

"Lovely evening, Reb Mendel," said someone who looked astonishingly like Sonia Nudelman, the mayor's wife.

Mendel continued walking, too amazed to even whisper hello in return.

Before long, he found himself in front of a house that looked remarkably like his own house. Children played in the front yard. They looked just like his very own.

"Papa, come play with us!" they shrieked.

And then the most amazing thing of all happened. A woman who was the spitting image of his own wife, Malke, leaned out the window of the small house and yelled in a loud, stern voice, "Mendel, where have you been all day? It's dinner time already and look at you, you're filthy. Come in, wash up. Children, come."

Mendel entered the house as if he was entering a dream.

"This house looks exactly like my own house back where I come from," he said.

"Mendel, what are you talking about? What do you mean, where you come from?" asked Malke.

"I have traveled a great distance. I have come from the small village of Chelm," said Mendel with a certain amount of pride.

"Oy, Mendel! Noodlehead! This is your home! You are from here!" sobbed Malke.

"How is it that you know my name, madam?" asked Mendel.

"How do I know his name, he asks? Nudnik! I'm your wife, Malke. We've been married sixteen years! Remember?"

"That's funny," said Mendel. "My wife back home is also named Malke. In fact, you even look like her. You could be her twin!"

"Ach, he's completely meshugga!" screamed Malke. "Help, somebody! Call a doctor! Call the rabbi! Just call somebody, quick!"

In a matter of moments, it seemed like the whole village of Chelm had crammed itself into the tiny house.

"I've never seen anything like it," grumbled the doctor when he had heard the whole story.

"Yes, a very tricky situation," commented the rabbi as he sat down stroking his beard, deep in thought.

After a few moments that seemed like hours, he cleared his throat and spoke. "Tell me, Mendel. If you are

here, where is the other Mendel that used to live here?"

"I suppose he must be in my home, back in my village," reasoned Mendel.

"In that case," continued the wise rabbi, "you should stay here until the other Mendel that used to live here returns. When he comes back to his home, you can return to yours."

So Mendel waited and waited many, many years for the other Mendel to return but, strangely enough, he never did.

Every now and then, Mendel thought about embarking on another journey, but he always decided against it.

"What's the point," he would always say to Malke. "If one place is exactly like every other place, one might as well just stay put."